MR. HAPPY
finds a hobby

Original concept by Roger Hargreaves
Illustrated and written by Adam Hargreaves

MR. MEN   **LITTLE MISS**
MR.MEN™ LITTLE MISS™ © THOIP (a SANRIO company)

Mr. Happy finds a hobby © 1998 THOIP (a SANRIO company)
Printed and published under licence from Penguin Random House LLC
This edition published in 2019 by Dean, an imprint of Egmont UK Limited,
The Yellow Building, 1 Nicholas Road, London W11 4AN

ISBN 978 0 6035 6771 1
70942/001
Printed in Great Britain

Egmont takes its responsibility to the planet and its inhabitants very seriously.
We aim to use paper from well-managed forests run by responsible suppliers.

DEAN

Mr Happy is a happy sort of fellow. He lives in Happyland which is a happy sort of place.

Behind his house there is a wood full of happy birds and on the other side of the wood there is a lake full of happy fish.

Now, one day, not that long ago, Mr Happy went for a walk down through the wood.

As he came to the shore of the lake he heard an unusual sound.

A sound that is seldom heard in Happyland.

It was the sound of somebody moaning and grumbling.

Mr Happy peered round the trunk of a tree.

At the edge of the lake there was somebody fishing.

Fishing and grumbling.

And grumbling and fishing.

It was Mr Grumble.

"Good morning, Mr Grumble," said Mr Happy.

"Ssssh!" ssshed Mr Grumble.

"Sorry," whispered Mr Happy. "Have you caught anything?"

"Yes! I've caught a cold!" grumbled Mr Grumble.

"I've been sitting here all night. I hate fishing!"

"Then, why are you fishing?" asked Mr Happy.

"Because Mr Quiet said it was fun! And, you see I'm trying to find something I enjoy doing. Something I can do as a hobby."

"Hmmm," pondered Mr Happy. "I might be able to help. Come on, let's see if we can find you a hobby."

As they walked along, Mr Happy thought long and hard and as he thought Mr Grumble grumbled.

He grumbled about the noise the birds were making.

He grumbled about having to walk.

But most of all he grumbled about not having a hobby.

Grumble, grumble, grumble.

First of all they met Mr Rush in his car. Mr Happy explained what they were doing.

"What's your hobby?" asked Mr Grumble.

"Speed!" said Mr Rush. "Hop in!"

And they did. Mr Grumble very quickly decided that he did not like going fast.

Next they met Little Miss Giggles.

"What's your hobby?" asked Mr Grumble.

"I...tee hee...like...tee hee...giggling," giggled Miss Giggles.

So they went to the circus to see the clowns.

Little Miss Giggles giggled, Mr Happy laughed and Mr Grumble...frowned!

"I hate custard pies," grumbled Mr Grumble.

It proved to be a very long day for Mr Happy.

They went everywhere.

They went to Little Miss Splendid's house.

But Mr Grumble did not like hats.

They went to Mr Mischief's house.

But Mr Grumble did not like practical jokes.

They bounced with Mr Bounce.

And they looked through keyholes with Mr Nosey.

But nothing was right. In fact, nothing was left.

Mr Happy had run out of ideas.

As the sun was setting, they saw Mr Impossible coming towards them down the lane.

"Now, if anybody can help us that somebody ought to be Mr Impossible," said Mr Happy.

"Hello," he said. "You're good at the impossible. Can you think of a hobby that Mr Grumble would enjoy?"

"That..." said Mr Impossible.

"Yes..." said Mr Happy and Mr Grumble together.

"...would be impossible," said Mr Impossible.

"Grrr!" growled Mr Grumble, and stomped off home.

It was whilst drinking a cup of tea the next morning that Mr Happy had an idea.

A perfectly obvious idea.

He rushed round to Mr Grumble's house.

"I've got it!" cried Mr Happy. "You can take up fishing."

"Fishing!? But I hate fishing."

"I know, but what do you do while you are fishing?" asked Mr Happy.

"I don't know."

"You grumble," said Mr Happy. "And what do you like doing most of all?"

"I like..." and then it dawned on Mr Grumble. "I like grumbling!"

Mr Grumble looked at Mr Happy and then for the first time in a very long time he smiled.

A very small smile, but a smile all the same.